This book belongs to

....

IMAGINE THAT™

Licensed exclusively to Imagine That Publishing Ltd
Tide Mill Way, Woodbridge, Suffolk, IP12 1AP, UK
www.imaginethat.com
Copyright © 2022 Imagine That Group Ltd
All rights reserved
0 2 4 6 8 9 7 5 3 1
Manufactured in Guangdong, China

ISBN 978-1-80105-326-6

5-minute
Magical
Christmas
Stories

Contents

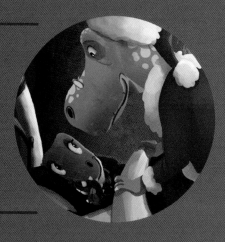

The Twelve Days of Christmas
Written by **Frederic Austen**
Illustrated by **Andrea Petrlik**

The Nutcracker
Written by **E. T. A. Hoffmann**
Retold by **Jamie French**
Illustrated by **Lucy Barnard**

We Wish You a Merry Christmas
Adapted by **Kitty Taylor**
Illustrated by **Paul Nicholls**

'Twas the Night Before Christmas

Written by
Clement C. Moore

Illustrated by
Marcin Nowakowski

'Twas the night before Christmas,
when all through the house

Not a creature was stirring,
not even a mouse.

The stockings were hung
by the chimney with care,

In hopes that St. Nicholas
soon would be there.

My sister and I were nestled
all snug in our beds,

While visions of sugar-plums
danced in our heads.

And mamma in her pajamas,
and father in his cap,

Had just settled down for
a long winter's nap.

When out on the lawn
there arose such a clatter,

I sprang from the bed
to see what was the matter.

Away to the window
I flew like a flash,

Tore open the curtains
and threw up the sash.

The moon shining onto
the new-fallen snow
Gave the luster of midday
to objects below.

When, what to my wondering eyes
should appear,
But a bright red sleigh,
and eight bright-eyed reindeer.

With a jolly old driver, so lively and quick,
I knew in a moment it must be St. Nick.

More rapid than eagles
his reindeer they came,
And he whistled, and shouted,
and called them by name!

"**Now**, Dasher!
Now, Dancer!
Now, Prancer
and Vixen!

On, Comet!
On, Cupid!
On, Donner
and Blitzen!

To the top of the porch!
To the top of the wall!

Now dash away! Dash away!

As dry leaves that before
the wild hurricane fly,

When they meet with an obstacle,
rising up in the sky.

So up to the house-top
the reindeers they flew,

With the sleigh full of toys,
and St. Nicholas too.

Then, in a twinkling,
I heard on the roof

The prancing and pawing
of each reindeer hoof.

As I drew in my head,
and was turning around,

Down the chimney
St. Nicholas came
with a bound.

He was dressed all in red,
from his head to his foot,

And his clothes were all tarnished
with ashes and soot.

A bundle of toys
he had flung on his back,

And he looked like a peddler,
just opening his pack.

His eyes—how they twinkled!
His dimples, how merry!

His cheeks were like roses,
his nose like a cherry!

His friendly mouth was
drawn up like a bow,

And the beard of his chin
was as white as the snow.

He had a broad face
and a little round belly,

That shook when he laughed,
like a bowl full of jelly!

He was chubby and plump,
a right jolly old elf,

And I laughed when I saw him,
in spite of myself!

A wink of his eye
and a twist of his head,

Soon let me know
I had nothing to dread.

He spoke not a word,
but went straight to his work,

And filled all the stockings,
then turned with a jerk.

And laying his finger
on the side of his nose,

And giving a nod,
up the chimney he rose!

He sprang to his sleigh,
to his team gave a whistle,

And away they all flew
like the seeds of a thistle.

But I heard him exclaim,
before he drove out of sight,

"Happy Christmas to all,

and to all a good night!"

Dino Claus

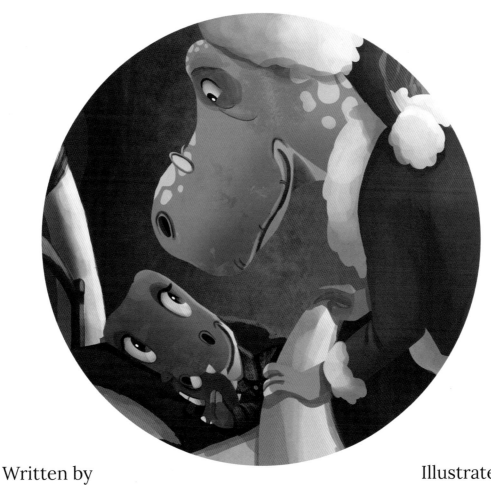

Written by
Susie Linn

Illustrated by
Adam Horsepool

It was December and everyone was excited about Christmas—everyone except Tiny, the little T. rex.

Tiny didn't believe in Christmas magic one little bit!

Daddy Rex loved Christmas more than anything! He couldn't wait to read his own favorite Christmas stories to Tiny at bedtime, but Tiny wasn't interested!

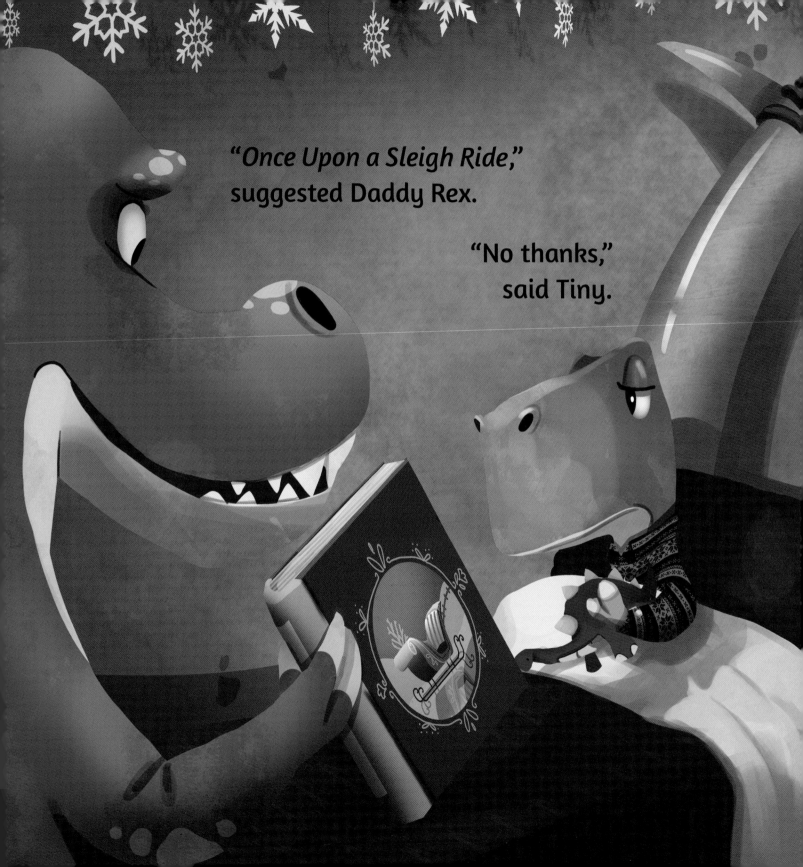

"Once Upon a Sleigh Ride,"
suggested Daddy Rex.

"No thanks,"
said Tiny.

"What about,
The Snowman that
Came to Life?" tried
Daddy Rex.

"No!"
grumbled
Tiny.

"You might like, *The Elves that Saved Christmas*," said Daddy Rex, hopefully.

Tiny said nothing.

He looked VERY cross!

"Maybe, *The Night Before Christmas?*" whispered Daddy Rex.

"No, NO, NO!" roared Tiny, grumpily.

On Christmas Eve, more snow began
to fall outside Tiny's cozy cave.
Suddenly, Tiny heard a jingling
and a jangling in the dark.
He heard the clatter of
hooves on rock!

Whoever, or whatever,
could that be?

Tiny peeped bravely out
at the entrance to his cave.

First, a brown furry
face appeared, then
some wiggly antlers!
Was that...
a reindeer?

Then a big sack,
bulging with presents,
landed on the cave floor!

Finally, a deep, jolly voice cried,
"Ho, HO, HO!"

A red hat with a white pom-pom appeared,
followed by the toothy, grinning face of big,
friendly...Dino Claus!

"Happy Christmas, Tiny!"
bellowed Dino Claus,
cheerfully. Tiny
just stared.

"I normally make sure no one sees me," continued Dino Claus, "but I heard that you don't believe in Christmas magic. It's time we had a chat."

Dino Claus answered all of Tiny's questions, until finally it was time for him to go.

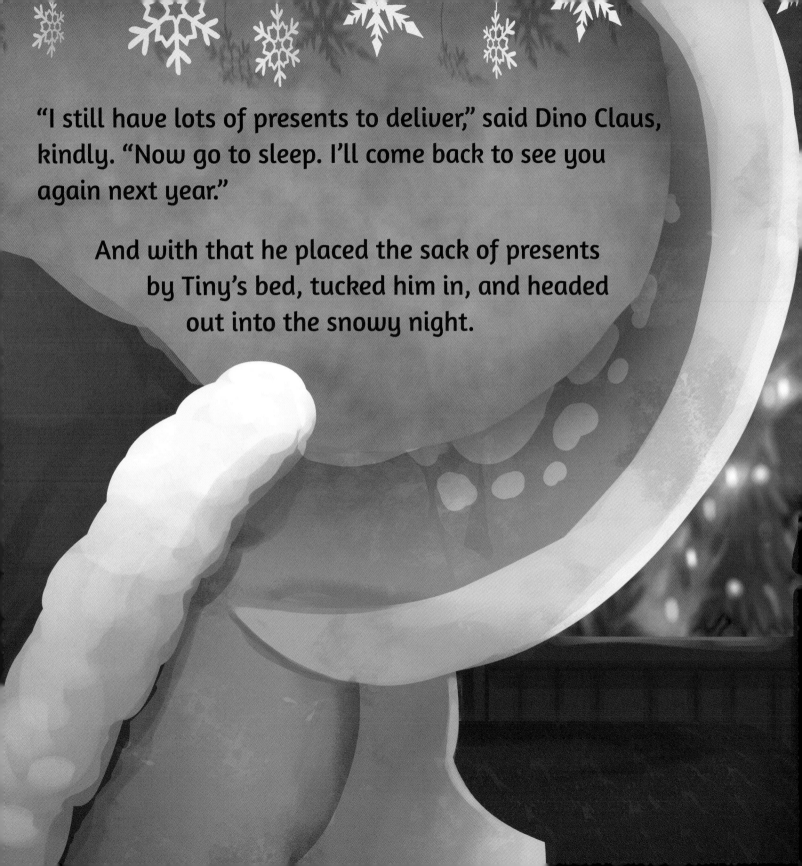

"I still have lots of presents to deliver," said Dino Claus, kindly. "Now go to sleep. I'll come back to see you again next year."

And with that he placed the sack of presents by Tiny's bed, tucked him in, and headed out into the snowy night.

Early on Christmas morning, Daddy Rex was woken by Tiny jumping on him, excitedly.

"Daddy! Look!" cried Tiny. "It's a book from Dino Claus!

It's called,
*The Most Magical
Christmas*. Can we read it, please?"

Daddy Rex grinned, wiped the sleep
out of his eyes, and began...

"Once upon a time, there was a little dinosaur who didn't believe in Christmas magic..."

Tiny cuddled up happily and sighed.

"I love Christmas,"
he whispered.

A Christmas Carol

Written by
Charles Dickens

Retold by
Joshua George

Illustrated by
Jennifer Miles

Scrooge was hard and sharp as flint!
The cold within him froze his old features,
and made his eyes red, and his thin lips blue.
He was a squeezing, wrenching, grasping,
scraping, clutching, and miserly man!

Scrooge's business partner, Jacob Marley,
had been dead seven years, but the
sign over the office door still said
"Scrooge and Marley."

It was Christmas Eve and Scrooge was busy at work.

Across the room, Bob Cratchit tried to warm himself at his candle. Scrooge was too mean to put more coal on the fire.

"Merry Christmas, Uncle!" cried a cheerful voice. "I am collecting money for the poor." It was Scrooge's nephew, Fred.

"Bah!" said Scrooge. "Humbug!"

"At least come for dinner with us tomorrow," said Fred.

"Bah!" said Scrooge again. "Humbug!"

At last it was time to close the office.
Bob Cratchit hurried home, but not before
stopping to slide down an icy hill.
It was Christmas Eve after all!

Christmas Eve was the same as any other day to Scrooge. His house was dark and dreary. Darkness was cheap, and Scrooge liked it.

As Scrooge sat alone he heard a strange noise, like someone dragging heavy chains up the stairs from the basement.

"Humbug," said Scrooge. "I don't believe it."

But Scrooge's face changed color when a familiar figure appeared!

"I am the ghost of Jacob Marley," cried the figure, clanking the chains it dragged behind it. "You will be haunted by three ghosts, Scrooge! The first when the clock strikes one..."

Later that night, Scrooge awoke to the "Dong!" of the church bell! Suddenly, the room filled with light and Scrooge found himself face to face with a strange figure.

"Who are you?" asked Scrooge.

"I am the Ghost of Christmas Past," said the figure. "Follow me."

The ghost showed Scrooge many Christmases from his past...

I was a boy here!

It showed him the Christmas when Scrooge was left to spend the vacations at school, all alone.

It showed him a Christmas party given by his first boss, Mr Fezziwig.

Old Fezziwig made us all so happy!

Finally, the ghost showed Scrooge the Christmas he left Belle, his one true love, to concentrate on making money.

Show me no more!

"Dong!" Scrooge woke in his bed again. When he opened the door to the next room, green leaves decorated the walls, and the loveliest Christmas foods were heaped on the floor.

In the middle of the food sat a jolly giant. "Come in!" boomed the giant. "I am the Ghost of Christmas Present!"

The second ghost showed Scrooge many different Christmases...

First it took him to Bob Cratchit's house. Although the Cratchits were poor, their little house was filled with happiness. "God bless us, every one," said the sickly-looking Tiny Tim.

Then the ghost took Scrooge to his nephew Fred's house. It was full of Christmas fun and laughter.

In every house they visited the ghost sprinkled the spirit of Christmas.

"Dong!" The church bell struck again and the Ghost of
Christmas Present disappeared.
In its place stood a tall, mysterious ghost,
wrapped in a black cloak. "Are you the
Ghost of Christmas Yet to Come?"
asked Scrooge. The ghost said
nothing, but just pointed forward.
"Lead on!" said Scrooge.
"I will follow you. Lead on, Ghost!"

The third ghost showed Scrooge Christmases that had not yet happened...

It showed him people talking about a man who had died. The man had been so mean that no one missed him.

My life is like his.

It showed him Bob Cratchit's house. Before it had been full of noise, but now it was quiet and Tiny Tim's little chair stood empty.

Poor Tiny Tim!

Finally the ghost took Scrooge to a churchyard and pointed to a grave. Scrooge crept, trembling, toward it and read his own name.

EBENEZER SCROOGE

I can change, I promise!

Scrooge woke and ran to the window. "What day is it?" he called to a boy outside.

"Why, Christmas Day!" replied the boy.

"Ha!" laughed Scrooge. "I haven't missed it! Merry Christmas everybody!"

Scrooge gave the boy money to buy the biggest turkey in the store. "I'll send it to Bob Cratchit's," he laughed. "It's twice the size of Tiny Tim!"

That afternoon, Scrooge went to dinner at his nephew's house. He was the perfect guest and joined in all the fun. And what's more, he gave a very large donation to the poor.

The next morning, Scrooge was at work extra early.

"You're late!" he growled, when Bob Cratchit arrived.
"I am not going to stand for this any longer...I am going to
raise your pay, and try to help you and your family, Bob!"

Scrooge was better than his word. He did it all, and much
more, and to Tiny Tim, who did NOT die,
he was a second father.

And so, as Tiny Tim said,
"God bless us,
every one!"

The Twelve Days of Christmas

Written by

Fredric Austen

Illustrated by

Andrea Petrlik

On the **FIRST DAY** of Christmas,
my true love gave to me...
A PARTRIDGE IN A PEAR TREE.

On the **SECOND DAY** of Christmas,
my true love gave to me...
TWO TURTLE DOVES,

And a partridge in a pear tree.

3

On the **THIRD DAY** of Christmas,
my true love gave to me...
THREE FRENCH HENS,

Two turtle doves,
And a partridge in a pear tree.

On the **FOURTH DAY** of Christmas,
my true love gave to me...
FOUR CALLING BIRDS,

Three French hens,
Two turtle doves,
And a partridge in a pear tree.

5

On the **FIFTH DAY** of Christmas,
my true love gave to me...
FIVE GOLDEN RINGS,

Four calling birds,
Three French hens,
Two turtle doves,
And a partridge in a pear tree.

6

On the **SIXTH DAY** of Christmas,
my true love gave to me...
SIX GEESE A-LAYING,

Five golden rings,
Four calling birds,
Three French hens,
Two turtle doves,
And a partridge in a pear tree.

On the **SEVENTH DAY** of Christmas,
my true love gave to me...
SEVEN SWANS A-SWIMMING,

Six geese a-laying,

Five golden rings,

Four calling birds,

Three French hens,

Two turtle doves,

And a partridge in a pear tree.

On the **EIGHTH DAY** of Christmas,
my true love gave to me...
EIGHT MAIDS A-MILKING,

Seven swans a-swimming,

Six geese a-laying,

Five golden rings,

Four calling birds,

Three French hens,

Two turtle doves,

And a partridge in a pear tree.

On the **NINTH DAY** of Christmas,
my true love gave to me...
NINE LADIES DANCING,

Eight maids a-milking,

Seven swans a-swimming,

Six geese a-laying,

Five golden rings,

Four calling birds,

Three French hens,

Two turtle doves,

And a partridge in a pear tree.

10

On the **TENTH DAY** of Christmas,
my true love gave to me...
TEN LORDS A-LEAPING,

Nine ladies dancing,

Eight maids a-milking,

Seven swans a-swimming,

Six geese a-laying,

Five golden rings,

Four calling birds,

Three French hens,

Two turtle doves,

And a partridge in a pear tree.

11

On the **ELEVENTH DAY** of Christmas,
my true love gave to me...
ELEVEN PIPERS PIPING,

Ten lords a-leaping,

Nine ladies dancing,

Eight maids a-milking,

Seven swans a-swimming,

Six geese a-laying,

Five golden rings,

Four calling birds,

Three French hens,

Two turtle doves,

And a partridge in a pear tree.

12

On the **TWELFTH DAY** of Christmas,
my true love gave to me...
TWELVE DRUMMERS DRUMMING,

Eleven pipers piping,

Ten lords a-leaping,

Nine ladies dancing,

Eight maids a-milking,

Seven swans a-swimming,

Six geese a-laying,

Five golden rings,

Four calling birds,

Three French hens,

Two turtle doves,

And a partridge in a pear tree.

The Nutcracker

Written by
E. T. A. Hoffman

Retold by
Jamie French

Illustrated by
Lucy Barnard

It was Christmas Eve and there was going to be a big party. The Christmas tree sparkled with lights and ornaments.

"It's so pretty!" cried Marie.

Soon, the guests arrived. The house was filled with music and dancing.

As Marie danced, a figure appeared in the doorway. It was Drosselmeyer, her godfather.

Drosselmeyer was a famous toymaker—
and he had brought gifts for everyone.

Drosselmeyer had an extra special gift for Marie. It was a wooden Nutcracker in the shape of a man.

Marie loved playing with her Nutcracker, but her brother was jealous. "It's not fair!" he cried.

Then he grabbed the Nutcracker and threw it across the room. *Crack!* went its head as it hit the floor.

Marie ran to pick up her Nutcracker, tears rolling down her cheeks.

Very carefully, she wrapped a ribbon around the Nutcracker's broken head. Then she placed him under the Christmas tree and went to bed.

Marie couldn't sleep so she crept downstairs to give her Nutcracker a hug.

As the clock struck twelve, something magical happened. Huge mice appeared from the corners of the room. And the Christmas tree started to grow!

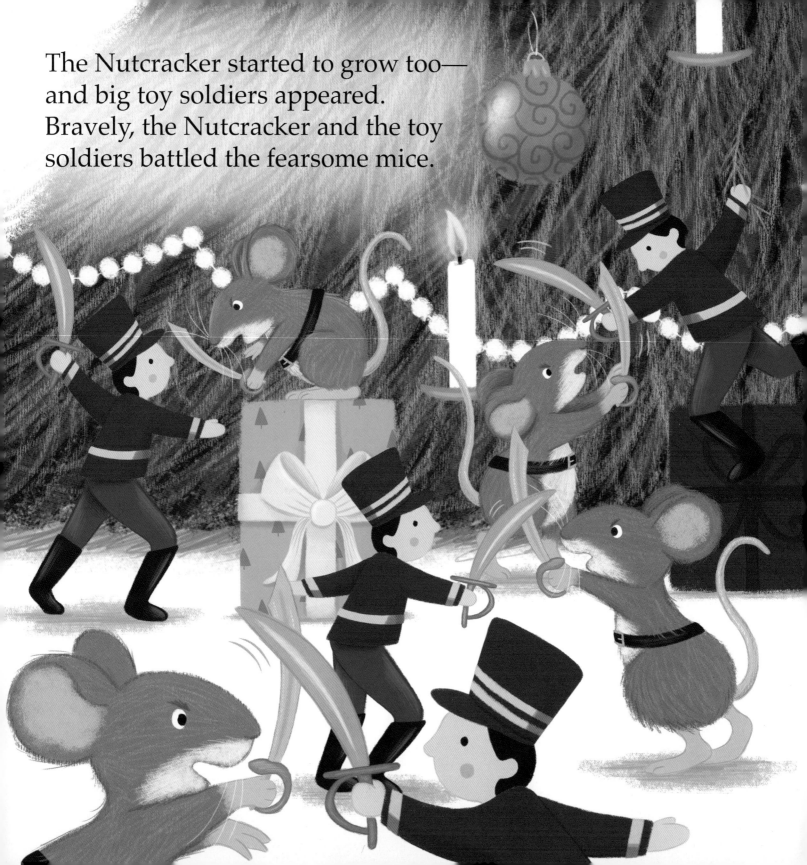

The Nutcracker started to grow too—
and big toy soldiers appeared.
Bravely, the Nutcracker and the toy
soldiers battled the fearsome mice.

"Look out!" called Marie, as the Mouse King attacked the Nutcracker. She threw her slipper at the mouse and he fell down.

The mice disappeared, beaten.

Suddenly, glittery snowflakes flurried around Marie,
and in the Nutcracker's place stood a handsome Prince.

"You have saved me," he said. "Come with me to my kingdom—the *Land of Candies*."

Marie and the Prince were greeted by
the pretty Sugar Plum Fairy. The Prince
explained how Marie had saved his life.

To celebrate, the Sugar Plum Fairy put on a dance show. Everyone was dressed as candies.

Soon it was time for the last dance.

As the Sugar Plum Fairy and her sweetheart danced for Marie and the Prince, a magical sleigh appeared to take them home.

"Remember me," whispered the Prince as they flew away.

Ding-dong-ding! went the Christmas Day bells. Marie awoke from the strangest dream and ran to pick up the Nutcracker. "I love you so much," she said.

And with that, the Nutcracker disappeared. In his place stood the Prince from Marie's nighttime adventure!

"Your love has freed me from an evil spell!" laughed the Prince, spinning Marie around and around.

Years later, Marie and her Prince got married—and went to live happily ever after in the *Land of Candies*.

We Wish You a Merry Christmas

Adapted by
Kitty Taylor

Illustrated by
Paul Nicholls

Merry Christmas!

We wish you a merry Christmas,
We wish you a merry Christmas,
We wish you a merry Christmas,
And a happy New Year.

Good tidings we bring
to you and your kin,
We wish you a merry Christmas
and a happy New Year.

Merry Christmas!

Now bring us some figgy pudding,
Now bring us some figgy pudding,
Now bring us some figgy pudding,
And bring some out here!

Good tidings we bring
to you and your kin,

We wish you a merry Christmas
and a happy New Year.

For we all love our figgy pudding,
For we all love our figgy pudding,

Merry
Christmas!

Hello
there!

For we all love our figgy pudding,
And lots of good cheer!

Good tidings we bring
to you and your kin,

We wish you a merry Christmas
and a happy New Year.

And we won't go until we get some,
And we won't go until we get some,

And we won't go until we get some,
So bring some out here!

Good tidings we bring
to you and your kin,

I love
singing!

We wish you a merry Christmas and a happy New Year.

We wish you...

...a merry Christmas...

We wish you...

...a merry
Christmas...

We wish you a
merry Christmas...

...And a **happy New Year!**